MAKING
Hand

BROOKE MUNKRES

authorHOUSE

AuthorHouse™
1663 Liberty Drive
Bloomington, IN 47403
www.authorhouse.com
Phone: 833-262-8899

Published by AuthorHouse 03/30/2023

ISBN: 979-8-8230-0294-3 (sc)
ISBN: 979-8-8230-0293-6 (hc)
ISBN: 979-8-8230-0295-0 (e)

Library of Congress Control Number: 2023904511

Print information available on the last page.

CONTENTS

THE MAVERICK

All I can see is the tail of the maverick bull that I am trying to catch!

My stomach is in my throat because I haven't roped a bull yet. I glance over at Colt to make sure he is still with me. In the back of my mind, I'm thankful I'm on Lil Man because I'm certain Colt will get to the maverick bull before me.

Colt is on his good sorrel gelding Patrick. Nothing has ever outrun Patrick and Colt is a good hand. I can see Colt closing in on the bull that Colt's dad, Lane, who's the ranch foreman, sent us to catch. Out of the corner of my eye I see Patrick jump something. Before I have time to process what it was, I feel Lil Man jumping.

I look down and see a deep arroyo and I'm right above the middle of it. I squeak because this arroyo is deep and wide. Thankfully before I have time to do more than squeak Lil Man has all four feet on solid ground again and is stretched out running as fast as he can after the bull. Colt is looking over his shoulder and is laughing at me. He must have heard the squeak I let out as Lil Man sailed over that arroyo. Colt doesn't laugh for long because Colt sees what I see.

The open desert land we've been tracking the bull across is about to end in a large thicket of trees. We both know it'll be the rest of the day getting the bull flushed out of there if he makes it to the trees. I see Colt over and under the end of his reins to push Patrick faster.

I thought Patrick was really running before, now he is flattened out and gaining on the bull with every stride. I'm in shock for a moment at how fast that soggy sorrel horse is before I realize I'm getting left in their dust and Colt will need help once he gets that bull roped.

I over and under my reins on Lil Man, asking for more speed. Surprisingly, my little, short cutting bred horse doesn't like getting left behind. Lil Man stretches out and is eating up some ground.

I get close enough to see Colt swinging his rope and roping that big bull around the neck. Colt slows Patrick down gradually once the rope comes tight, so Patrick doesn't have to take such a hard jerk to stop the bull.

I ride up as Colt gets the bull slowed down to a walk. The bull weighs close to one thousand pounds and is on the fight. Colt always ropes tied on instead of dallying. I always love seeing Colt and Patrick work a rope tied on. It's an art I haven't gotten brave or experienced enough to try YET.

As I ride up Colt starts riding Patrick out to the side of the bull trying to give me a shot to ride up and rope the bulls two back feet. I'm riding around toward the back of the bull, giving him room so I don't get him even more on the fight while Cole is turning the bull and giving me an opening.

As Colt turns the bull to give me a heel shot, the bull charges! Colt turns Patrick and is getting out of the way when I kick Lil Man up into position for a heel shot. I swing and throw.

I see my loop in slow motion wrapping around the front of the bulls back legs and as he steps into it with both back feet. I pull the slack out of my rope and quickly dally it around my saddle horn as I pull back on Lil Mans reins and sit deep in the saddle. My loop closes around both back feet and Lil Man buries his rear into the ground.

Lil Man takes a hard jerk as the weight of the bull brings the rope tight and takes both back legs out front under him. I look up and see Colt has his rope tight and the bull goes down.

Colt is smiling from ear to ear and we both just sit there to let our horses blow. Colt reaches behind his saddle to get a pair of cow hobbles he keeps tied there and steps down.

Patrick keeps the rope tight as Colt walks up to the bull and slips one side of the hobbles onto one of the bulls front legs then waves me forward to loosen the rope so he can get a back leg out of the loop. He slides the other loop of the hobbles over one of the bull's back legs.

Colt throws my rope free of the bull and as I'm coiling my rope, Colt signals to Patrick with a whistle and Patrick walks up to Colt, loosening the neck rope. Colt takes his loop off the bull. He gives Patrick a rub on the forehead and then coils his rope and hangs it back on his saddle.

Colt says "Let's let our horses blow some before we trot back to the truck to get the trailer. We will have to lead the bull across the arroyo, but we can bring the trailer just on the other side. We won't have to lead him more than a couple of miles."

I step off Lil Man and loosen my cinch so he can catch his breath easier. I rub his neck as Colt is loosening Patrick's cinch. He walks over says "You did good heeling him while he was running after Patrick and me. You are already making a hand."

As we rode back to the truck to bring the trailer closer to the arroyo we didn't talk. We loosened cinches again once we got to the trailer and loaded the horses.

Colt drove the truck and trailer about four miles to a game trail that had cut through the banks of the arroyo. We could lead the bull down and back up the other side to the trailer.

As we unloaded the horses and tightened up our cinches, I asked Colt, "Has a bull ever been gone when you got back to them when you tied them down?"

Colt chuckled and said "yeah that's why I use cow hobbles now. Less likely for them to be gone when I don't have to tie a knot in a tie string." When we got in sight of the bull, and he was still lying there, I was relieved that we didn't have to run and catch him all over again.

Colt got off Patrick and laid a loop over the bull's head. He backs Patrick up until the rope is tight and then waves for me to ride over. I ride up and hand him my loop and he slips the hobbles off the bulls back foot and puts my loop around one back foot.

I back Lil Man up and we hold the rope tight as Colt finishes taking the hobble off the bull's front foot. He walks to Patrick and ties the hobbles back to his saddle then steps on.

I squeeze Lil Man to move him up to let my rope get some slack and Colt rides right up to the bull's head. He is standing beside the bull when he realizes it's not tied anymore. The bull gets up it lunges for Patrick.

I quickly dally and turn Lil Man around and ride off. I jerk the bulls back foot out from underneath him and he goes down again.

The next time the bull gets up Colt has the bull snubbed up short and the bull's head is next to Colt's leg.

The bull tries running over Patrick and I snug up the heel rope to stop him from running over Patrick and Colt.

Colt eventually points Patrick in the direction of the trailer with the bull pushing Patrick around. After taking a hard shove in the shoulder Patrick pins his ears back and paws that bull right between the eyes.

The bull finally quits shoving Patrick around after that. Then we get to the arroyo.

Colt says "I'm gonna slide my rope as I go down this trail until the bull is behind me. You just keep driving him and if he gets frisky just dally and slow him down."

I nod as Colt points Patrick onto the narrow game trail and slides rope to let the bull follow in single file down to the bottom of the arroyo.

I'm following close behind the bull and when it gets to the trail that leads down, he just stops. Colt and Patrick are jerked to a halt halfway down the trail and Patrick slides a foot or so backward as the bull starts backing up. Colt slides more rope and Patrick gets settled.

I point Lil Man at the bulls back end and bump the bull with Lil Mans chest as Patrick and Colt continue on down the trail and not sliding any more rope.

The bull lurches forward for a couple of steps until it feels the heel rope get tight then it slowly walks down the rest of the way following Patrick. Before I get to the bottom Colt has already got Patrick started up the opposite game trail with the bull following along behind.

I am following the bull up when suddenly he starts shaking his head and bellows. The bull is sliding and pulling back on the rope and I look up to see Patrick digging in for all he's worth but still getting drug back down the bank of the arroyo.

Colt is trying to pull his dallys free so he can slide rope, but they got caught and now he's tied on hard. I quickly ride Lil

Man up behind the bull and take the end of my rope and swing. I aimed for the one spot that I knew would get that bull moving. My aim was surprisingly good, and I hit that bull square in the balls with the knot on the end of my rope.

Things happened quickly after that. The bull lurches forward and is running right on Patrick's tail the rest of the way up that bank. Lil Man and I are right on the bulls heels in case the bull decides to charge Patrick again once it gets to the top. When I get to the top of the trail, I dally to slow the bull down.

We just stand there for a minute and give our horses a chance to blow. The trailer is right there and after our horses have had a minute to catch their breath Colt rides over to the back of the trailer and opens the gate. Then he swings the rope over a ball that is welded to the top of the trailer on the drivers side. The bull is facing the open trailer and colt rides up so his rope is tight. When Colt and Patrick start pulling, I ride up behind the bull and swing the end of my rope again to encourage him to load in the trailer. The bull loads up and I jump off Lil Man to shut the cut gate behind him. Colt rides up to me as I'm getting the chute hook, long metal pole that has a hook bent into the end so we can get our ropes off the bull. I get Colts rope off first as he is stepping off Patrick and then he helps me get my rope off the heel.

We loosen our horses cinches and load the horses into the back of the trailer. On the way back to the ranch, Colt looks over at me and asks "hey you did good out there Bella. Can I ask how you got that bull to run up that bank so quick though?" I grinned and said, "I smacked him in the balls with the knot end of my rope."

Colts' eyes got big and then he starts laughing. "That'd sure do it. You're making a hand Bella."

THE GATHER

I'm riding my roan mare, Roanie, and Colt is on his good sorrel ranch horse, Patrick. Lane, the ranch foreman and Colt's dad is riding his bay gelding, Skip. A couple of Colt's friends Flint and Will are also helping us gather. Flint is riding his good sorrel mare, Patricia and Will is riding a young bay gelding, Rash. We are long trotting in a single file line to the back of the South pasture.

This week we are gathering cattle for the spring works. We have already gathered all the other pastures and have all the pairs in smaller traps that are closer to the headquarters.

At spring works we ear mark, brand, castrate and vaccinate. A couple of the neighboring ranches will be here to help.

Lane is leading the way and then Colt, Will, Flint and I'm bringing up the tail. The counts have been correct for the other sections that we have gathered so we haven't missed any cattle so far. This pasture should have 150 pairs of momma cows and calves.

As we get to the back of the pasture, Lane starts dropping us off. He says "Bella!" and I veer out of the single file line and hold up and wait for the others to get dropped off one at a time until we all form a long and spread-out line.

We are slowly gathering any cattle we see in front of us toward the gate that we left open when we came into this pasture. It leads to a trap that is much smaller than the pasture they are currently in. As we are walking, we make sure we keep even so we keep everything moving in front of us.

I spot a handful of momma cows with their calves, and they start trotting ahead of me with their calves close to their sides. This country is rough with not a lot of grass, so it takes a lot of land to sustain 100 pairs. I keep pushing the cattle ahead of me and keep an eye out for any others in my line of site. The old cows have been through many gathers and know they will get fed once we get to the smaller trap, so they are moving off and headed toward the trap.

All the momma cows have had their babies by now and the few that lost them during birth or after, have already been separated and are back in with the bulls or have been sold. I make sure all the mommas in front of me have their babies with them, so we aren't leaving any babies behind.

I keep an eye on Flint and sometimes see Will in the far distance when he or I go on top of a rise. It is still early morning as it helps ensure we don't leave any calves behind because most of them have just fed from their mommas after being bedded down during the night.

I've now got 30 pair moving out at a leisurely walk in front of me. I ride up on a rise and I can see Flint with just as many pair that he is pushing in front of him.

As I crest the rise I see a new momma join the bunch I'm pushing but I don't see her calf. The momma is pacing and circling while she is bawling for her baby. Her bag is swollen so her calf hasn't fed yet today. She lets the other pairs pass her and she keeps pacing around in the same area.

As I ride near her she gets on the fight and charges Roanie. As I'm getting out of her way I hear a calf bawling. With the momma hot on my heels I can't see where the calf is at so I ride back up to the top of the rise and wave my hand in the air for help. I catch Flint's attention and he makes my direction to come help me.

When Flint rides up he asks "What's up Bella?" I reply "There's a mad mamma down there that doesn't have her calf with her. She's on the fight but I heard a calf bawling from somewhere. I just can't check it out with that cow trying to eat Roanie for lunch. Can you please draw that cow away as I check on the calf?" "Sure thing Bella." Flint says.

As we ride back down to the distraught momma cow Flint rides towards her and when the cow chases him, he leads her away in a large circle. As soon as they are well away, I ride up to the area the cow was pacing and hear a calf bawl. There is no calf in site though. The bawling sounds like its coming from under the ground!

I look up to make sure Flint is still leading the cow away and when I see they are a safe distance but slowly curving back toward me, I step off Roanie and ground tie her.

There is a large patch of sage and when I walk near it the calf bawling gets louder. As I was through the sage, I see a deep hole. When I peek over the edge of the hole, I see a little white face peaking up at me. The calf is half buried and all that I can see are its head and neck. All of a sudden, I hear Flint hollering "Get back on your horse Bella!" I jump back away from the hole and run for Roanie!

When I get to Roanie I see Flint and Patricia is running fast with that very mad momma cow right on her tail! I pick up my reins and jump on Roanie. I turn her and get out of the way just in time for Patricia and Flint to go running by me with that cow still hot on their heels!

He turns Patricia to take the mad momma on another circle and says, "Make it fast Bella!"

I kick Roanie up into a lope toward the patch of sage and we slide to a stop near the edge of the hole. I jump down and grab my rope. I tie the tail of my rope to my saddle horn and jump down in the hole with that calf. I hurry as fast as I can to dig the front legs of the calf out of the sandy dirt so I can put my loop around them and have Roanie pull the calf out.

I can hear Flint cursing at the mad momma cow and telling me to hurry. Just as I get the second leg free, I hear hooves getting close. I quickly put my loop around both front feet of the calf and use the rope to climb out of the hole. I can see Flint and Patricia headed back our way and I jump up in the saddle and turn Roanie.

I don't have time to worry about anything else as Roanie leans into the weight of the rope and starts walking away from the hole. I can't see the calf, so I don't know how its doing but its coming out. Roanie pulls with everything she has and then she walks off like a weight has been taken off the rope.

I look back to see the calf being drug though the sage on its belly. Roanie continues pulling the calf until its out of the sage and then I turn around and trot back towards the calf to take my rope off. I jump off Roanie, jerk my rope off the calf's front legs and then turn to jump back in the saddle as I see Flint and Patricia coming in fast.

Just as I get in the saddle Patricia runs by me and I kick Roanie into a run with her. The calf bawls and the cow leaves us to go check on her calf. The cow starts licking the calf and soon the calf is back on its feet. It's a little wobbly but its up and walking.

Flint stops Patricia and asks me "Where was that calf?" I rode over to the hole and showed him. I said "The calf was ¾ of the way buried and I had to dig its front feet out so I could have Roanie drag it outta there. I sure appreciate your help distracting that momma. She was on the fight for sure."

Flint looked at me and then shook his head. He said, "It's a good thing you found it cause that calf wouldn't have made the night with all these coyotes out here." He patted Patricia's neck and said "Come on, I'll help you push these two and catch up with the others."

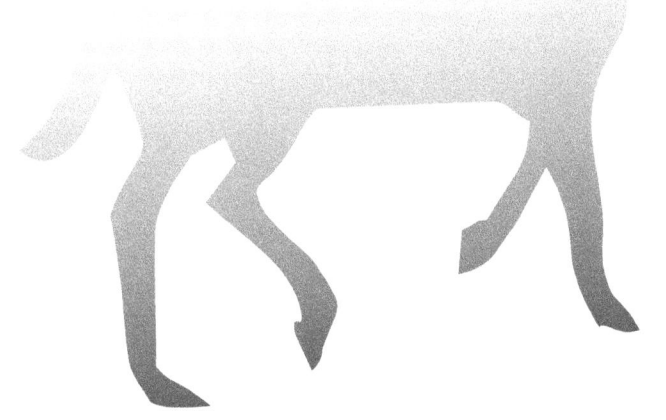

THE BRANDING PEN

Today is the third and final day of sorting and branding calves. I usually give shots to calves that Colt and the neighboring ranch hands drag to us.

Then, after lunch the hands that have been the ground crew all morning take over roping and dragging calves.

I'm not nearly as dirty as some of the other ground crew. The two guys that throw the calf down to the ground are the dirtiest, Rex and Shorty. They are also the biggest guys. Rex is over six feet tall and weighs probably 250. He's in his mid thirties and has a large belly over hanging his belt.

Shorty is not much taller than my 5'5" height but he looks like he goes to the gym more than he works out on the range. He is pale skinned, that has turned a bright red since being here and has blingy jeans on. He is new to the neighboring ranch so maybe he just hasn't had enough time to toughen up. He struggled the first day of helping Rex throw calves but he's got it now and is doing a good job. I haven't seen him horseback yet.

Another neighboring ranch hand, Josh, castrates bull calves. He's average height, a little under 6' and has the long sinewy muscles of a cowboy. He's quiet and doesn't talk much when I'm around.

The foreman, Lane, brands the calves on the left ribcage. The brand is a spur with a big rowel on it.

Lane looks like an older version of Colt. He's around 6' tall with the lean muscle of a cowboy. He has a handlebar mustache, and his skin is like leather. Tan and wrinkled. He's a good boss and seems fair.

At lunch I see Shorty walk over to Lane, who is sitting on the tailgate of his truck eating his lunch. Colt and I are sitting across from him on Colt's tailgate.

Shorty says "Sir I'd like to drag this afternoon if that's ok with you?"

I haven't seen Shorty horseback yet and didn't even know he had a horse here.

Lane shrugs his shoulders and says "Sure Shorty. You've done enough rolling around in the dirt the last couple days."

After lunch is over, Lane comes over to Colt and I and speaks to Colt. "Son, I want you dragging this afternoon too. You, Bella, and Shorty will drag." Colt nods and says "yessir".

As lunch wraps up everyone starts walking back to the pens.

I walk over to Lil Man and tighten up his cinch and take his hobbles off.

Just as I step up into the saddle, I see Shorty step up on a rangy, skinny colt that has a spooked look in his eye.

That colt has a hump in his back when Shorty steps on, but it takes Shorty's kick to the ribs and moves forward when he asks.

Colt, Shorty, and I ride into the pen and start building a loop once the ground crews are ready. There are three sets of ground crews. One for each dragger.

I'm dragging to Josh and Rex and another neighbor hand named JT has taken Shorty's place tailing calves. JT's wife, Brit is now giving shots and notching ears.

I've drug 7 and Colt has drug 10. I've seen Shorty catch a few but don't know how many. His colt still looks jumpy but he's handling him and getting his job done.

It's a couple hours later and we are getting down to a handful of calves left to drag. We left a few momma cows in with all the calves to keep them settled. Now the calves are hiding behind the momma cows and getting harder to rope.

Colt catches two hind feet on a calf that is running down the fence in front of him.

He jerks his slack and keeps his hand in the air as he turns his horse and trots off toward his crew. He's got his rope shortened up but is tied off. As he gets father from his calf, he lets the rope slide through his hand and when he reaches the end of his rope the calf falls and he drags him to the crew.

I sidle Lil Man up to one of the momma cows and reach over her back swinging my loop. She moves and gives me a shot at the calf that was hiding behind her. I catch two hind feet and jerk my slack as I'm turning Lil Man towards Rex and TJ. I trot off as I'm dallying and the calf falls. I don't get far before I see, in slow motion, Shorty caught a calf by one back leg and when he turns his rangy colt towards his crew that calf takes off around the back of his horse.

The rope comes tight. Unfortunately the calf has caught that rope under the tail of the colt. Rim fired!

The colt clamps his tail down on the rope and drops his head to the ground as all four feet come off the ground. Shorty is trying to stay on his bucking horse while popping his dallies.

He gets his dallies popped and drops the tail of his rope. That calf is running in the same direction as the colt is though and the rope is still clamped down under its tail.

Everyone sees what's happening at once and scatters out of the way as the colt makes a bee line straight for the back gate.

The crew, coolers of medicine and the branding fire are all in his way.

Colt's crew and Lane are working his calf and as Colt spurs his horse forward, he hollers "MOVE!!!" His flankers and the rest of the crew run for the fence.

My crew isn't far behind. TJ is keeping Brit in front of him as they run for the fence as Rex brings up the rear.

Shorty's crew is heading for the opposite fence closest to them.

I pull Lil Man up and pop my dallies.

I let my rope come loose and the calf gets up and runs back to the momma cows and few calves that are left to work.

The calf that Shorty roped turns and heads back to the group of calves and momma cows also.

It jerks the rope out from under the colts tail and I'm hoping the colt stops bucking.

It's on a roll though and it is full out bucking now that the rope is out from under its tail.

Shorty is still holding on but he's getting looser in the saddle with every jump.

The colt runs through all the coolers with medicine in them and sends them flying.

It's headed for the fire!

Right before it reaches the fire, I see Colt charging towards them.

Shorty is about to be airborne when Colt rides up beside him and grabs him under the arm.

Shorty reaches for Colt and grabs him around the waist. Colt pulls his horse up and the colt bucks right out from under Shorty.

Shorty lands on his knees with his hands in the dirt.

We all watch as the colt continues bucking straight through the middle of the fire. Scattering coals and embers.

I kick Lil Man up and run up to help Colt catch the loose horse.

I ride up to the left side of the horse and Colt rides up to the right. We keep him in a straight line as he bounces off Lil Man and Colt's horse. I grab the reins and dally them to my horn. I make a sweeping turn to the left as Colt keeps him pressed up against Lil Man.

The colt finally stops bucking and I pull him down to a stop.

I look up and see medicine bottles broken and coolers dumped on their side. The branding fire is smoldering with the few coals that are left in the fire ring.

The crews start heading back in to assess the damage and set up to continue the works.

Lane is looking at the bottles of medicine to see if there is enough unbroken bottles to finish the works. He doesn't look happy.

Colt looks at me and says "Thanks for the help Bella"

He takes the colts reins from me and leads him up to Shorty, who is slowly walking over to us with a red face.

Colt hands him the reins and says "You alright?"

Shorty replies "yeah, I appreciate the help."

Shorty walks over and ties his horse to the fence to help clean up the mess that his bronc ride caused.

Lane walks over to him where he is picking medicine bottles out of the dirt and claps him on the shoulder. "Shorty, you need to go ride that colt. Don't worry about all this. By the time you get done lining him out we will be ready to drag calves again."

Shorty looks embarrassed and reply's "I don't mind cleaning up the mess I made sir. I can work him after we are done working today."

Lane shakes his head and reply's "No you go get that horse lined out and we will get everything put back together. Go on now son."

Shorty nods and say's "Yessir".

He walks over and unties his horse and takes him outside the pens into the pasture. When he steps up into the saddle the colt starts humping up again, but Shorty spanks his butt with the end of his reins and takes out at a fast lope away from the pens. I watch until he goes over a rise and disappears as I'm picking up medicine bottles.

I put the unbroken ones back in the cooler and pick up the broken bottles and throw them in an empty feed sack on back of the feed truck that we are using as a trash can.

By the time we are ready to drag calves again, Shorty is back to the pens on a sweaty colt that looks to have had a proper attitude adjustment.

Lane tells Shorty to get in there and help Colt and I drag the last few calves.

I keep an eye on Shorty and the colt as we rope our first calf. The colt is tired and seems like an honest citizen from there on out.

After all the calves are worked and paired back up with their momma's, Lane say's "Colt and Bella, take these pairs to the East pasture. We will save you some supper at the ranch house for when you get back."

Colt just nods and say's "We'll swap out our horses for fresh ones and then we will get going." He nods to me, and we both take our horses over to the barn to swap our tack onto fresh horses.

It'll take two hours to get the pairs over to the East pasture. It'll take half that to get back to the ranch.

It's already six o'clock so it looks like it will be another late night tonight.

Thankfully, all we have to do tomorrow is feed and doctor the couple cows that we held back in the sick pen and check to make sure all the pairs are still paired up.

It's been a long week but branding is one of my favorite parts of the job.

THE BLIZZARD

It is -10 and blustery outside this morning. Colt and I are getting ready to ride our horses out to the West pasture closest to the ranch to check on cows. It's a week before Christmas and yesterday a blizzard blew in and hasn't left. Before the blizzard hit we hauled round bales of hay out to all the cattle but still need to check water and bust ice few times a day.

It's a job getting out to the cattle but it has to be done. We both carry axes on our saddles to bust ice.

The snow is almost belly deep to our horses and a ride that normally takes us 20 minutes in the summer will take us 2 hours today. Our horses are up in the barn now and get free choice hay and extra grain to keep the weight on them. I grab one of the ranch geldings that makes up part of my string.

His name is Pata, meaning Legs in Spanish. Pata is a great horse for big circles and covering lots of country. He has a lot of go and is rangy. He watches where he puts his feet in rough country. Pata stands a little over 16 hands and is leggy. He isn't great in the pens because he doesn't have the quick feet to make that fast turns that Lil Man does but he's smooth to ride and has a lot of heart.

Colt catches his big dun horse named Bronc. Bronc is a big draft cross that came out of a bucking horse string from a local rodeo contractor. Colt bought him because he was tough and works great for times like this. We call Broncs kind rock mashers because they are big and tough enough to mash rocks.

It takes Colt and I both to open and close the barn doors so we can lead our horses out.

It is hard to step up in the stirrup with all these clothes on. I've got four layers of clothes on underneath my bibs and the heaviest coat I own over the top. I'm wearing my mud boots because they are insulated.

The snow is deep and the going is slow. Colt and I both put our heads down and he leads the way to the closest pasture. Flint and Lane have already headed out to the farthest pasture to bust ice and check on the bulls.

Colt leads the way after we go through the gate. Bronc and Pata fall into a slow pace and we make a beeline for the closest pond.

After 30 minutes of slow walking we arrive at the first pond. It's hard to see but Colt didn't take too long to find it. We both step down off our horses and get our axes. We trudge through the deep snow towards the pond. It is sheltered from the worst of the wind by several trees around the perimeter. It is a short reprieve from the biting wind and the horses are able to get a break while Colt and I bust holes in the ice for the cattle. As we are chopping ice we can see and hear cattle taking shelter from the storm in the trees.

When we finish making several holes for the cattle to drink from we both step back up in the saddle and ride through the herd to make sure the cattle are doing all right. This is the first of 3 pastures that we need to get to today.

The cattle are huddled together with their backs to the wind when we find them. They are in the most heavily wooded area and seem to be fairing pretty well. We put hay out just before the storm hit and created a bit of a wind block from the worst of the wind with the bales. Some cows are bedded down in the hay and seem all of them are accounted for.

We start out for our second pasture at the same slow walk. My skin is all covered except for my face around my eyes. I try to keep my head down to block most of the wind from reaching my uncovered skin.

When we reach the second pond we repeat the same process. The horses are starting to sweat from working so hard walking through the deep snow. We don't want them to stand too long so we hurry to chop the holes in the ice.

I hear the cattle in the trees again and we check to make sure they are all accounted for.

They are doing the same as the cattle in the first pasture and are all accounted for.

The last pasture we need to check has the replacement heifers in it. These are the young females that we are keeping back to breed and replace the older cows that get sold off. They are not bred yet.

When we get to the last wooded area that surrounds the post we chop ice them remount our horses to check on the heifers. Since they aren't bred and are fat they should be doing just fine. As we are riding through the herd and counting them we see some that are bedded down in the hay next to the wind block and others are standing with their backs to the wind. Colt waves at me and I ride over to him.

He has to yell for me to hear him. He yells "Do you hear that?" I pick my head up and listen. I'm startled when I faintly hear a calf bawling. I look at Colt and yell over the wind "I hear a calf!" Cot nods his head and takes off in the direction that we heard the sound coming from.

We are in a low draw of trees that is in between to large hills on each side.

WE follow the draw and weave our way in between trees. The brush is thick but the snow is not as deep in the woods. Suddenly I see Colt kick Bronc into a run and he's crashing through brush like a bulldozer.

I kick Pata into a lope and follow Colt and Bronc. Pata doesn't crash through the brush like Bronc does though. He jumps the low brush and I have to pay attention so I don't get my head taken off by a low hanging limp. Soon Colt pulls Bronc up and jumps off.

As I draw Pata up I see what got Colt in such a rush.

A cow from the next pasture has gotten into the heifer pasture and given birth early.

The cow is still down and isn't trying to get up. The calf is up and still bawling. It is a very large calf. She must have had a hard time delivering such a large calf.

I jump down from Pata and cringe when my cold feet hit the ground. My feet hurt from being so cold.

Colt is already do'wn and checking on the cow. The wind is calm so far down in this draw and I hear him curse when he walks to the back end of the cow.

As I walk up to the calf I ask him "what happened?". He says "She pushed so hard to get that big sucker out her uterus is prolapsed."

Colt walks back to Bronc to get his pistol to put her out of her pain and I check the calf. He's still wet from the birth and is shivering.

I quickly take one of my undershirts off without shedding any outer clothes and start wiping the big guy off to get him dry, He is too weak still to put up much of a fight and ends up falling over while I'm vigorously rubbing him down.

I startle when I hear the gunshot go off and the calf clumsily jumps to his feet.

I keep ahold of him and look up when Colt walks back to Bronc to put his pistol back in his saddle bag. He gets his sat phone out and I hear him call his dad. "Hey dad. Theres a cow from the second section pasture here in the heifer pasture. I figured you were looking for her. She had a really big calf and prolapsed her uterus and I had to put her down. Yeah, I'll bring it back to the house. See ya there."

After Colt put his sat phone back in his saddle bag he walks over to the mostly dried but weak and cold calf and me and says "I'll pack him back on Bronc if you will help me get him up there."

I nod and hold the calf still while Colt leads Bronc closer to the calf. When Colt reaches us he picks the calf up while I hold Bronc still. When Colt goes to put the calf up in front of the saddle so he can get on Bronc snorts and sidles away. Bronc is not happy about packing a calf! After a few more tries with no success Colt looks at me and says "Will Pata pack this calf?"

I say "Pata has a lot of go but he's never been spooky of anything and is a pretty honest citizen. It'd be worth a shot."

I walk over and get on Pata. Colt walks up to him slow carrying the calf and lets him smell it.

Pata smells it then gives in a lick.

Colt mmoves slowly and lifts that big calf up into my lap. He then slips one of his undershirts off from under his outer clothing and covers the calf with it. Colt takes my wet shirt and shoves it into my saddle bags,

As Colt is stepping up on Bronc the calf decides it doesn't know about riding a horse on my lap and gives a few good kicks to Patas shoulders and neck. Thankfully all Pata does is rise his head a bit but stands still.

Colt starts heading back out of the draw and into the freezing wind again to get back to the ranch as quickly a possible.

Soon after Pata starts walking the calf gives another few kicks but Pata just walks as fast as he can through the deep snow. He knows the way home and is ready to get back to his warm barn.

CPSIA information can be obtained
at www.ICGtesting.com
Printed in the USA
BVHW041248210423
662799BV00001B/3